This book belongs to

_____

An Octopus Came for Tea

By Nadia Mulara

for my babies

A Mermaid Swam

in the deepest Sea.

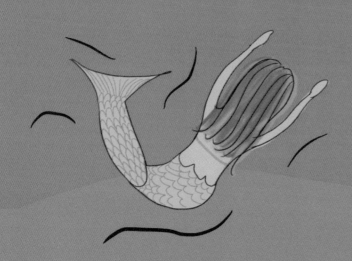

Inviting her friends to come for...

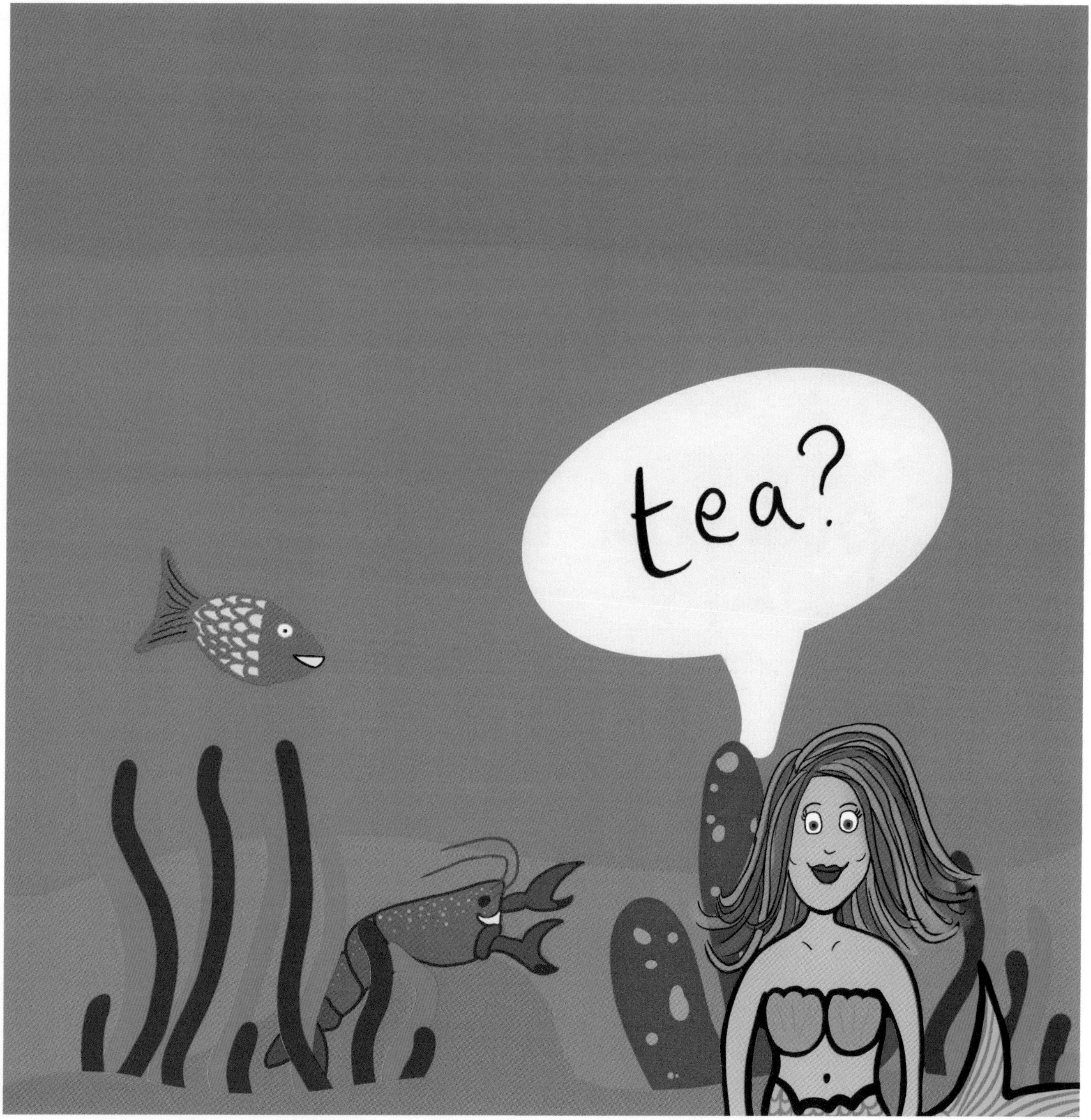
tea?

On her travels she

passed a Sad

Octopus.

And said "Hey there,
Why don't you have
tea with us?"

With a smile he gave his eight arms a shake.

The mermaid hoped she would have enough cake.

They laid the table
with all kinds of
treats that everyone
would like to eat.

The fish and the lobster ate fish cake and eel, then thanked the mermaid for the tasty meal.

The guests were having so much fun and there was plenty of food for everyone.

The mermaid told the Octopus "I thought you'd eat it all".

The Octopus replied
"Well I have only got
one mouth afterall".

What rhyming words
did you hear?

Did you see Jungle Pants?

What page was he on?

Can you decorate your own teapot.

Other books from the
Ocean Adventures series

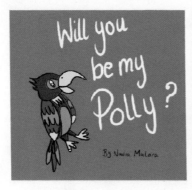

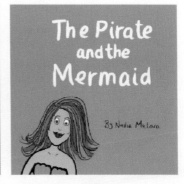

More books by Nadia Mulara

Available on Amazon now

Check out author_nmulara on Instagram for competitions and updates on new books

Printed in Great Britain
by Amazon

83512848R00020